IT HAPPENED IN CHELM

A STORY OF THE LEGENDARY TOWN OF FOOLS

RETOLD BY
FLORENCE B. FREEDMAN

ILLUSTRATED BY
NIK KREVITSKY

SHAPOLSKY PUBLISHERS
NEW YORK

IT HAPPENED IN CHELM
A Story of the Legendary Town of Fools

Published by Shapolsky Publishers
136 West 22nd Street, New York, New York 10011
212 / 633-2022

ISBN 0-944007-00-7

Library of Congress Cataloging-in-Publication Data

Freedman, Florence B. (Florence Bernstein)
    It happened in Chelm : a story of the legendary town of fools /
retold by Florence B. Freedman ; illustrated by Nik Krevitsky. —
1st ed.
        p.   cm.
    Summary: The inhabitants of the mythical mid-European town of
Chelm consult their Town Council of seven wise men when their shops
are robbed by bandits in the night.
    ISBN 0-944007-00-7. — ISBN 0-933503-22-9 (soft)
    [1. Humorous stories.]   I. Krevitsky, Nik, ill.   II. Title.
PZ7.F872771t   1989
[Fic] — dc20   89-24160
                                                                    CIP
                                                                    AC

Design and Typography by Stephen Romaniello
First Edition, 1990

To all people of all ages, everywhere,
in all times who love
to tell,
to hear, and
to read
stories.

TO THE READER:

I heard my first Chelm story when I was about eight years old, and I loved to hear it again and again. Now that I am ten times that age I still like tales about Chelm.

After you have read this one I think you will know why so many people have enjoyed these Chelm stories for so many years.

Chelm is a town of fools, but they are lovable fools. They are never mean; they don't play tricks on people; they never lie. They always work together to solve their problems, often with the help of their seven wise men.

They try to solve their problems in imaginative ways. Because the full moon gives so much light, they capture it in a bucket of water so that it will give light when the nights are dark. Because the town is in a valley between two mountains, and they need more space, they work hard at pushing the mountains farther away.

The newly fallen snow is so beautiful that they don't want it spoiled by the footsteps of the shammos as he goes to summon the men to prayer, so they have him carried by four men.

And when they need a watchman . . . well, you'll find out what happens when you read this book.

Maybe we enjoy these stories because there is a little bit of Chelm in each of us. I know there is in me.

Florence B. Freedman

On a hill, high above the town of Chelm, somewhere in the middle of Europe, every night from sundown to sunup, sits a lonely man, wearing a sheepskin coat, astride a horse that never moves.

He is the town watchman.

Why is he there, so far from the town he is supposed to protect? Well, if you must know, it is because Chelm is a town of fools.

How all the fools came to live in one town - the town of Chelm - is another story. But there they were, living happily, raising children, hens, cows, and sheep, selling and buying to and from each other in their shops, and praying twice each day, and almost all day on Sabbath and holidays in their synagogue.

It was only when they had to plan something, or think about something, or explain something, or solve a problem, that an outsider could tell that the Chelmites were fools. But since people were too polite to tell this to the Chelmites, they lived on as we all do, from day to day, from hand to mouth, and as God wills.

Whenever the Chelmites had a problem too difficult to solve, they went to their Town Council of seven wise men. (Even fools have their wise men, as everybody knows).

No, I haven't forgotten about the watchman, sitting up there on the hill. He came to be there because of a terrible catastrophe.

One morning when the shopkeepers came to their shops, they found the doors open and the shelves bare. In the shoemaker's shop there wasn't a pair of boots or a piece of leather. The tailor had no coats, no pants - even a new suit for a bridegroom was gone. Only a few scattered nails remained on the floor at the blacksmith's. There wasn't a cupful of flour at the mill. Not a single herring floated in the grocer's barrel, and not even one small potato lay in his bin.

The Chelmites knew immediately what had happened. Bandits had swooped down from the hills in the middle of the night, and had robbed every shop.

What a tragedy! The Chelmites had hardly enough for themselves; they couldn't supply the needs of the bandits as well!

The shopkeepers went to the seven wise men, and presented their problem.

How could they prevent such a thing from happening again?

The seven wise men deliberated

for seven days and seven nights.

Then they sent for the shopkeepers and presented their decision.

"S-i-n-c-e," they began in the sing-song which always accompanied a point of logic, "the shops were robbed at night when they were closed, and s-i-n-c-e they were never robbed in the daytime when they were open, we therefore advise as follows: keep the shops open at night, and closed in the daytime."

"What logic!" said the shopkeepers admiringly. "Only the seven wise men of Chelm could have thought of such a solution. They have heads of pure gold."

But one thing was wrong with the advice of the seven wise men. When the shopkeepers kept their shops open at night while the other Chelmites were asleep in their beds, the bandits did not come - but neither did the buyers. And even a Chelmite knows that no one can sell if no one buys.

The wise men were respectfully asked to find another solution. After seven days and seven nights, they summoned the shopkeepers.

"S-i-n-c-e the bandits come by night, and since the shopkeepers want to sleep at night, the best solution is to find someone who will watch the shops at night and let the shopkeepers sleep in peace - in short, you should hire a watchman."

The shopkeepers knew just the man - Zalman, who was big and strong, and who lived alone, so that it did not matter if he slept by day or by night.

Zalman was proud to become the first and only watch-man of Chelm. But every new plan brings new problems, at least it does in Chelm.

Where was the watchman to stand?

"Near my shop," said the shoemaker. "It's the nearest to the hills where the bandits live. If he stands by my shop, Zalman will catch them before they do any damage."

"True, your shop is nearest to the hills it's nearest to," said the tailor. "But suppose other bandits come from the opposite hills. They would come to my shop first. Zalman should stand near my shop."

"I have a compromise," said the grocer. "My shop is in the middle, Zalman could get to either end if he stood near my shop."

The argument almost turned into a quarrel, as often happens with fools. Before they came to blows, however, they went to consult the seven wise men.

Promptly at the end of seven days and seven nights, the wise men sent for the shopkeepers. "S-i-n-c-e the watchman is hired by all the shopkeepers of Chelm, and s-i-n-c-e it wouldn't be fair to have him protect one shop more than another, we suggest that he stand on a hill above the town, equally distant from all the shops."

"Such logic! Such justice! Truly the heads of the seven wise men are pure gold," said the shopkeepers, and they hurried off to decide together where Zalman should stand. It was a Monday night when Zalman began to watch the town from high on the hill.

On Tuesday morning he came down shivering and shaking and blue with cold. The shopkeepers revived him with a glass of steaming tea with a slice of lemon and a spoonful of strawberry preserves in it.

"It's freezing up there," Zalman complained. "I can't stand it."

"We'll get you a warm coat - a sheepskin coat. Will that help?"

That very night Zalman, splendid in his sheepskin coat, climbed the hill, ready to watch the town.

In the morning he came down, again shivering and shaking - this time not from cold, but from fright.

"All night the wolves were howling at me. They smelled the sheepskin coat, and thought I was a sheep they could slaughter. One came so close I could see his murderous eyes. Some night they'll kill me. You can't reason with a wolf!"

This was a problem for the wise men, who because of the urgency of the case - a man's life in danger, God forbid - deliberated seven times as fast as usual and had an answer the very next morning. The shopkeepers, in turn, took immediate action, and when Zalman was ready to go up the hill, they had a high and bony horse for him to ride.

But nothing is ever perfect. Zalman was almost as afraid of the horse as he had been of the wolves. "I've never ridden a horse. He'll run away with me!" Zalman moaned. "Then what will you do for a watchman?"

"Do you think we'd let anything happen to you?" the shopkeepers reassured him. "We'll tie the horse to a tree so that he won't be able to run away."

Night after night Zalman, snug in his sheepskin coat, sat safely astride the horse who was tied to to a tree. The watchman watched, the sleepers slept, and the bandits . . . being bandits, they had to strike again!

One morning the shopkeepers found every door broken
and every shelf bare. Not a shoelace, not a nail, not a scrap
of cloth or a cupful of flour was left.

Fortunately, however, the watchman seemed to be in good health.

"Zalman, Zalman, what happened?"

"Why didn't you stop the bandits?"

"Where were you?"

"Where should I be?" asked Zalman, aggrieved. "I was right where you told me, up on the hill, where I'd watch the town."

"You saw the bandits?"

"Of course!"

"Why didn't you chase them?"

"My horse was tied to a tree."

"Why didn't you untie him?"

"I can't ride. You know that. He could have run away with me!"

"Then why didn't you get off the horse and run after the bandits?"

"I was afraid the wolves would smell my sheepskin coat and think I was a sheep and kill me."

"Why didn't you take off the coat?"

"And freeze?" Zalman was shocked. "After all, you gave me the coat to keep warm. And such a fine coat! Do you think I'd sacrifice such a coat to the wolves?"

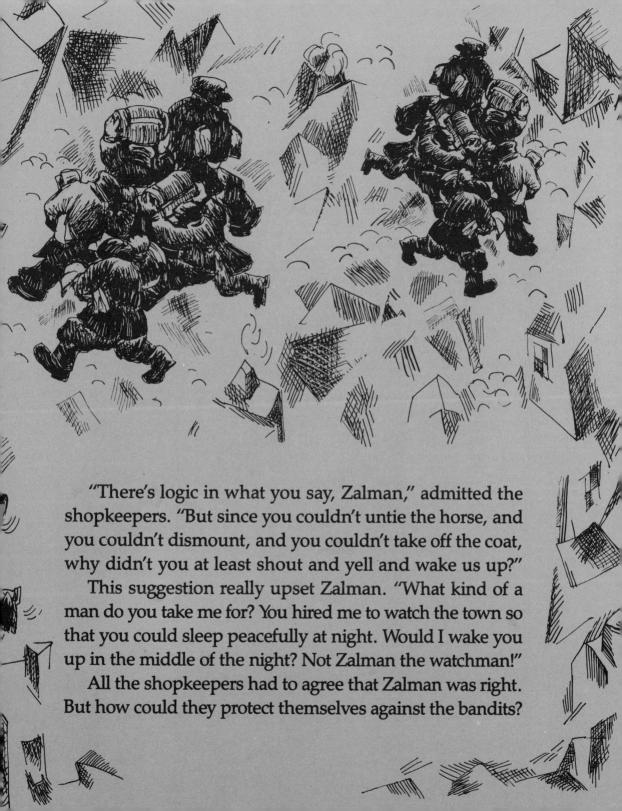

"There's logic in what you say, Zalman," admitted the shopkeepers. "But since you couldn't untie the horse, and you couldn't dismount, and you couldn't take off the coat, why didn't you at least shout and yell and wake us up?"

This suggestion really upset Zalman. "What kind of a man do you take me for? You hired me to watch the town so that you could sleep peacefully at night. Would I wake you up in the middle of the night? Not Zalman the watchman!"

All the shopkeepers had to agree that Zalman was right. But how could they protect themselves against the bandits?

The shopkeepers again brought their problem to the seven wise men, who deliberated for seven days and seven nights,

and another seven days and seven nights,
and still another seven days and seven nights.

For all I know,

they are still deliberating . . .

In the meantime, high on a hill

overlooking the town of Chelm,

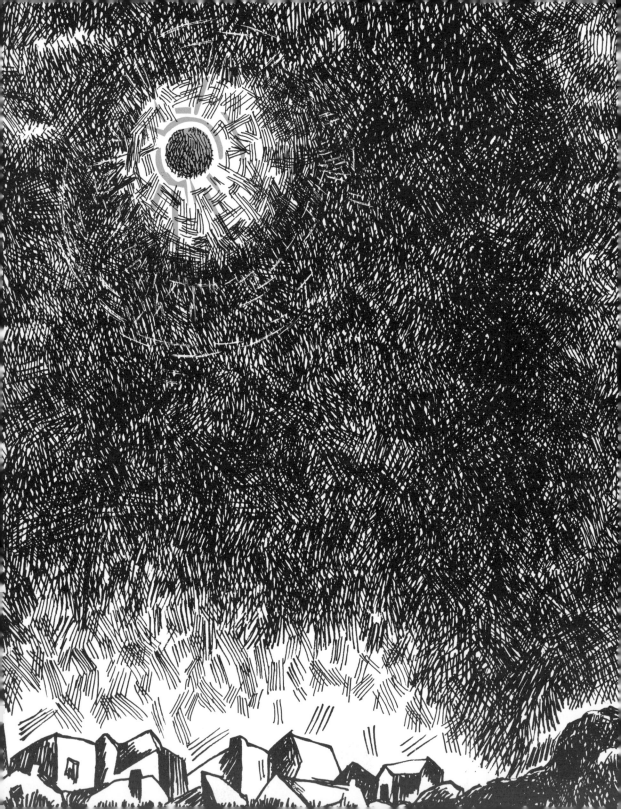

sits a watchman wearing a sheepskin coat

astride a horse that never moves.

It is the faithful Zalman watching over the town

so that all the Chelmites can sleep

peacefully in their beds.

Florence B. Freedman was born in Brooklyn and spent most of her life there and in New York City. Beginning her career as a high school teacher of English and Hebrew, she joined the faculty of Hunter College in 1952 and retired as Professor Emeritus in 1972. Her writing includes poems, some reprinted in anthologies, and books relating to Walt Whitman, the subject of her doctoral dissertation. In 1985 her scholarly book, *William Douglas O'Connor, Walt Whitman's Chosen Knight* was published by University of Ohio Press.

It Happened in Chelm is Dr. Freedman's third book for young people, following *Two Tickets to Freedom, the True Story of Ellen and William Craft: Fugitive Slaves*, 1972, republished 1989 by Peter Bedrick Books, and the prize-winning *Brothers: a Hebrew Legend*, 1985, Harper and Row.

Florence Freedman shares her children's stories with her six grandchildren.

Nik Krevitsky, well-known exhibiting designer-craftsman, has spent much of his career in art education. He was born in Chicago and attended the Universtiy of Chicago. For many years he has lived in Tucson, Arizona, where the unique desert ecology is his constant inspiration.

Among Nik Krevitsky's published works are *Batik: Art and Craft, Stitchery: Art and Craft,* and *Shaped Weaving,* all published by Van Nostrand Reinhold. *It Happened in Chelm* is Nik Krevitsky's first venture into children's book illustration. It is a natural result of a long-time friendship with the author whom he met when they both were Doctoral candidates at Columbia University. His calligraphy appears in *November Journey,* a collection of Florence Freedman's poems published in 1973, their first collaboration. Along with his current involvement in children's literature, Dr. Krevitsky is now doing experimental print-making.